W9-BSK-995

To Edi
~ Love, Juli

Written by JULIA COOK

Illustrated by ANITA DuFALLA

Boys Town, Nebraska

Tease Monster

ISBN 978-1-934490-47-1

Published by the Boys Town Press
14100 Crawford St.
Boys Town, NE 68010

For a Boys Town Press catalog, call **1-800-282-6657**
or visit our website: **BoysTownPress.org**

Publisher's Cataloging-in-Publication Data

Cook, Julia, 1964-

Tease monster : a book about teasing vs. bullying / written by Julia Cook ; illustrated by Anita DuFalla.
-- Boys Town, NE : Boys Town Press, c2013.

p. ; cm.
(Building relationships ; 3rd)

ISBN: 978-1-934490-47-1

Audience: grades K-6.
Summary: When "One of a Kind" is laughed at by Purple One and called a name by Green One, is the Tease Monster to blame? This tale teaches readers the difference between friendly teasing and mean teasing, and why some teasing can have a negative bite if it's meant to be hurtful and cause embarrassment.--Publisher.

1. Children--Life skills guides--Juvenile fiction. 2. Teasing--Juvenile fiction. 3. Bullying--Juvenile fiction. 4. [Success--Fiction. 5. Teasing--Fiction. 6. Bullying--Fiction.] I. DuFalla, Anita. II. Series: Building relationships ; no. 3.

PZ7.C76984 T43 2013

E 1302

Printed in the United States
10 9 8 7 6 5 4

Boys Town Press is the publishing division of Boys Town, a national organization serving children and families.

My name is

"One of a Kind."

People might think that all "ones" are alike, but there isn't another "one" out there just like me.

I **LOVE** to eat banana popsicles

upside down while standing on my

head.

I'm made up of many different

colors.

I can ride a unicycle and play the accordion at the same time.

My feet are so big that
I only wear shoes when I
absolutely have to.

Oh, and when I eat pizza,
I always eat the crust first!

Who does that?

I really like being me, but being a one isn't always easy. Sometimes the other ones aren't very nice, and they

TEASE *me!*

The purple one, who's older than me,
made fun of the way I eat.

She said my colors were

weird,

and she laughed at my

great big feet.

The other ones started to laugh at me too, and agreed with what she said.

I felt so bad all I wanted to do was spend the rest of my life

in bed.

When our teacher walked by, the laughing stopped
and the ones just walked away.

But the way they made me **feel inside**

completely ruined my day!

Then after that, my best friend Green
did something to me that was really **mean!**

When I tripped on the stairs on my way back from lunch,
she laughed at me and called me a
klutz.

I felt so bad when she called me that name.
It wasn't my fault...
my big feet were to **blame!**

That afternoon, when our math tests came back,
the plaid one called me a

brainiac!

"When it comes to math, you're like a machine!"
He sounded all nice, but to me, it was mean!

When I got home from school, I told my mom how rotten my day was.

"I hate being teased, it's no fun at all!
I'd rather be plastered right into a wall!

I'm not going back…
I'll do school from home.
I don't even care
if I'm home all alone!"

“Sounds like you’ve been bitten by the Tease Monster!” my mom said. “Dealing with the Tease Monster is just a part of life.

Every one teases and every one gets teased, so the sooner you learn how to deal with it, the better off you’ll be.”

"There are two types of teasing:

the **NICE**

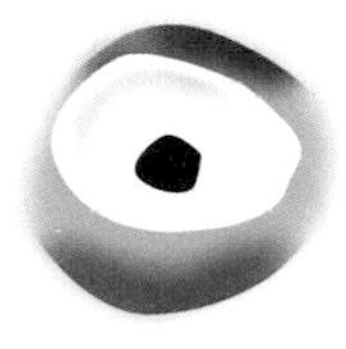
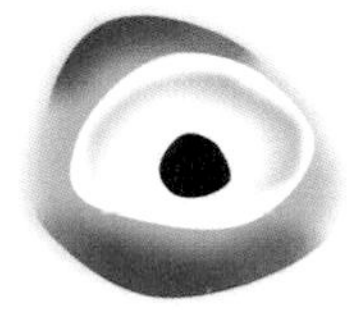

and

the **MEAN.**

You think every one's against you,
but it's not like it seems.

You must learn the difference
between each kind of bite,

Because not every tease
takes away from your life."

"What's the difference?" I asked.

"Well," said my mom. "It's just like math!"

"A **MEAN** *tease bite is negative (-),*
and it takes away from your life.
It divides you in half,
and can even make you cry.

Mean teasing is bullying,
and it's not a good thing.
The ones that do it
are trying to be mean.

It's a mean tease bite when it comes from some one who doesn't care about you and wants to embarrass you or make you feel bad on purpose."

"A **NICE** *tease bite is positive (+),*
and it adds to your life.
It multiplies your strength
and your voice that's inside.

It can help you solve problems
in humorous ways.
It can get you through life
on the not-so-great-days.

A nice tease bite comes from
some one who cares about
you and would not want to
hurt you or make you feel bad.
Nice tease bites are good because
they can help you build better
relationships with other ones."

"Purple's tease bites are mean,
and she's trying hard to hurt you.
She does it because she wants power,
and she doesn't care what you go through.

Whenever she tries to single you out,
stay calm and ask her to stop.
If that doesn't work, stay out of her way,
and avoid her at all costs.

If Purple keeps mean teasing, and still won't stop,
then you'll need to go ask for some help.

Find a grown-up to talk to that you can **trust**
so you don't have to feel like you've felt."

"Green's bite was a happy, nice tease,
when she said that you were a klutz.
She'd never try to hurt you, because
she likes you way too much!

When she called you that name,

she was laughing **WITH** *you.*

Nice teasing is **FUN,**
and it can help you get through…

the tough times in life,
like when you trip over your feet.
But a smile and a nice tease
can make the tough times more sweet."

"Plaid wasn't mean teasing.
He said what he said...
to compliment you
for something you did.

His nickname for you
was harmless and fun.
You're a very smart kid,
and a **WONDERFUL ONE!"**

Just then, my little brother rode into the kitchen on my old unicycle, hanging onto the wall for dear life. He accidentally pedaled into a chair, lost his grip, and went "SPLAT" on the kitchen floor.

"What a GOOF!"

I said!

He looked at me with a tear in his eye.
"I'm not a GOOF!" Then he started to cry.

"GEEZ, what a baby!"

I thought to myself.
I wasn't being mean; I just said what I felt.

"You always tease me, and it makes me feel rotten!
I came in to show you how good I have gotten!"

My mom hugged my brother and made him stop crying.

She said,

"You can do it!

Just never stop trying!"

My brother got back on the unicycle, grabbed onto the wall again for dear life, and pedaled out of our kitchen.

"You need to be careful
about what you say.
A nice tease bite to you,
can ruin his day.

Sometimes when you nice tease,
your words go too far.
You just have to realize
how powerful they are."

"How do I do that?" I asked.

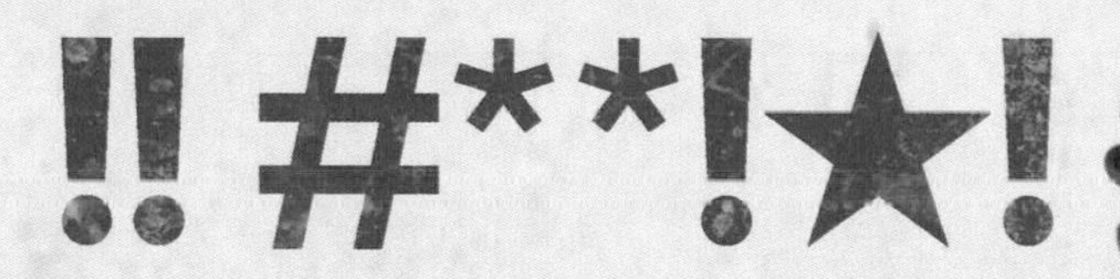

"First of all,
my **One-of-a-Kind,**
just think about what you say.
Once other ones hear the words you speak,
you just can't take them away."

"You can always pretend
to look into a mirror
and practice your words on yourself.

Do you like what you're hearing?

Are your words hurting others?

Or are you saying things that can help?

Pay close attention to the look in the eyes
of the one you are talking to.
Are your words making the one's eyes smile,
or are you making that one feel blue?"

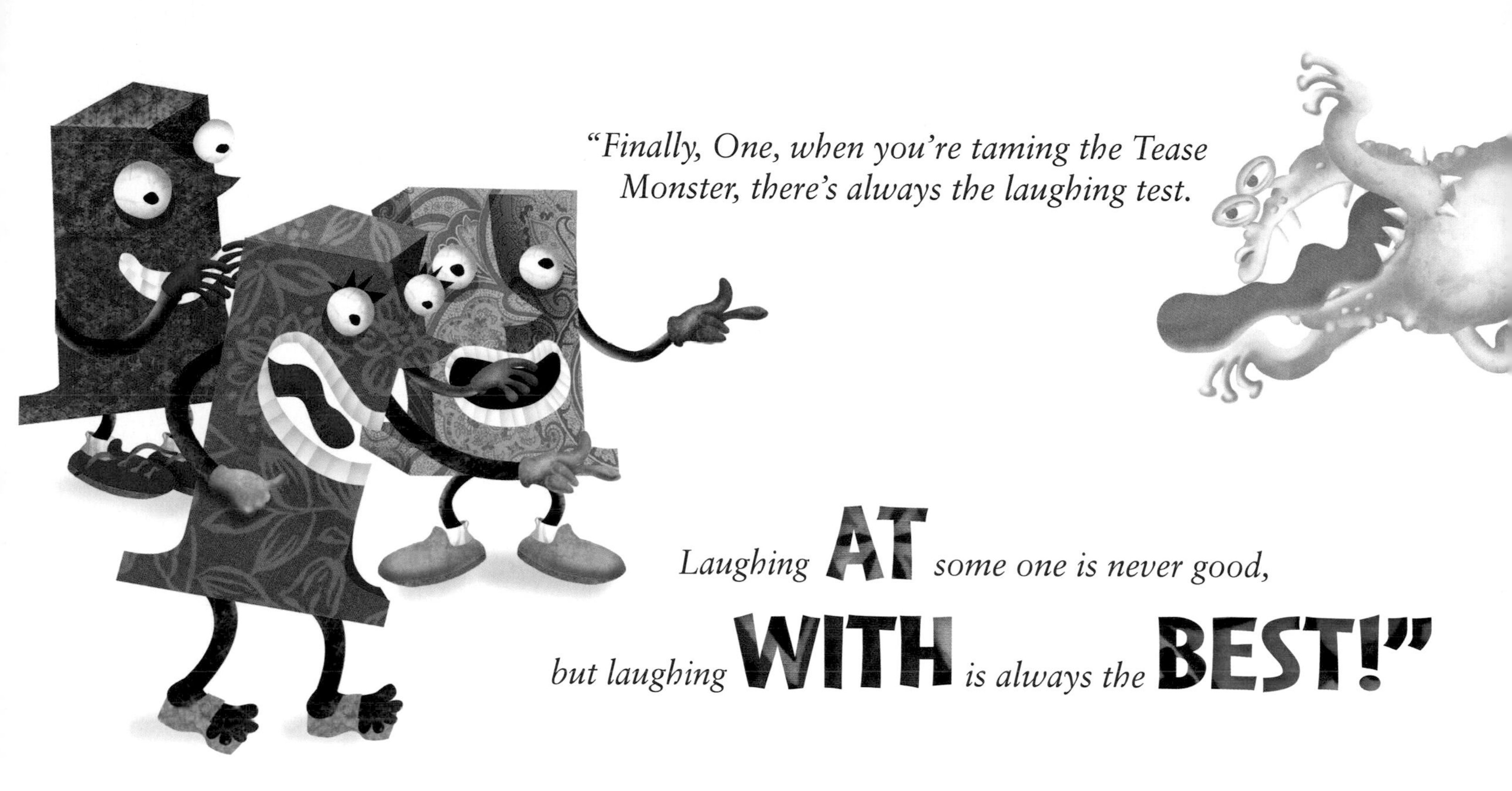

"Finally, One, when you're taming the Tease Monster, there's always the laughing test.

Laughing **AT** *some one is never good,*

but laughing **WITH** *is always the* **BEST!"**

Today, I thought about everything my mom taught me about the Tease Monster, and my day at school was quite a bit less rotten.

I tried my best to stay out of Purple's way, but when she started teasing me at lunch about the way I eat my pizza,

I smiled at her with **my eyes,**

picked up my tray, and changed tables!

During art, I made myself laugh when Green accidentally spilled her paint all over my paper. Then I told her that we could start our very own

"Klutz Club for Ones,"

and she laughed WITH me!

I told Plaid that I would help him with his math if he would stop calling me brainiac in front of everyone, and he promised never to do it again.

And, when I got home,
I told my little brother

how **proud** I am of him

for being **brave**
enough to get on a unicycle!

...I sure hope he doesn't start
taking accordion lessons!

Now that I know
how the Tease Monster works,
I now know that some words
are not meant to hurt.

It's always a good thing
to watch what I say,
and understand every one
hears things different ways.

Teasing's not all bad,
and most times it's fun,
as long as you

laugh WITH
and **NOT**
AT any ONE.

"Here, want a banana popsicle?"

Tips for Parents and Educators

Teasing is a human social exchange that can be perceived as friendly, neutral, or negative. The goal of teasing should be to create closer relationships and make connections. Pro-social teasing helps to satisfy a fundamental human motivation – to be an integral part of a group. It has its benefits: Teasing can be playful, help to promote social affiliations, allow people to better deal with awkward situations, and help to bring both the teaser and the person being teased closer together. Teasing turns into bullying when kids use it to gain greater social status, or when the intent of what is said or done is to harm. **The best way to learn how to deal with teasing is to better understand it. Here are a few tips:**

- Teach your child how to tease and accept teasing through body language, laughter, and sarcasm, so that he/she can see the differences between a serious and joking interaction.
- Define the differences between teasing and bullying with your child: Teasing creates stronger relationships while bullying damages relationships. Teasing adds to your character as a person while bullying takes away from your character. Teasing occurs between equals (age, power, intelligence, friendships) while bullying occurs between people who are unequal. Teasing maintains dignity or respect toward a person while bullying is done to embarrass or hurt the feelings of a person. Teasing may include harmless nicknames that the target also thinks are funny. Calling a target names that are derogatory or directed at his or her religion, ethnicity, speech, appearance, etc., is bullying.
- Listen to your child without disagreement. If your child tells you that one of her classmates said her clothes are ugly, don't jump in and reassure the child that her clothes are beautiful. If you do that, you infer to your child that she has been victimized. Instead, listen carefully to what your child is telling you, and then work with her to come up with a plan to address this situation the next time it happens.

Teach your child how to respond when teasing turns into bullying:

- Remain calm, but serious.
- Assertively ask the person to stop the bullying behavior.
- If the behavior does not stop, ignore the person or remove yourself from the situation.
- If the behavior stops, thank the other person for stopping and explain how the behavior made you feel.
- Report continued bullying or hazing to an adult at school and an adult at home that you can trust. If you don't want to tell them in person, write them a note. Signing your name on the note can be optional.

For more parenting information, visit boystown.org/parenting.

BOYS TOWN. Parenting

Boys Town Press Books by Julia Cook

Kid-friendly books to teach social skills

978-1-934490-86-0

978-1-934490-97-6

978-1-934490-30-3

978-1-934490-39-6

978-1-934490-47-1

978-1-934490-48-8

978-1-934490-62-4

*Reinforce the social skills RJ learns in each book.**

978-1-934490-43-3

978-1-934490-49-5

978-1-934490-67-9

Other Titles: The Worst Day of My Life Ever!, I Just Don't Like the Sound of NO!, Sorry, I Forgot to Ask!, and Teamwork Isn't My Thing, and I Don't Like to Share!

**Accompanying posters sets and activity guides are available.*

978-1-934490-76-1

978-1-934490-76-1

Other Title: Well, I Can Top That!

978-1-934490-98-3

978-1-934490-80-8

978-1-934490-90-7